Whirlwind is a Spirit Dancing

Poems based on Traditional American Indian Songs and Stories

ILLUSTRATED BY **LEO** AND **DIANE DILLON**
TEXT BY NATALIA BELTING
EDITED AND INTRODUCED BY JOSEPH BRUCHAC

Distributed by Publishers Group West

INTRODUCTION

The poems in this collection are based on traditional American Indian songs, stories and folk beliefs. To really understand these poems, you need to understand one simple truth: In the eyes of Native Americans, everything in the natural world is alive. The wind, the moon, the sun and the stars are all seen as living beings. Not only that, these living beings are aware of human beings and are responsive to prayers, songs, and ceremonies.

This belief is one reason why Native Americans try to live in a balanced way with their environment. If everything in the natural world is aware of your actions, you are more likely to show respect to that world.

These stories and traditions taught people not only to appreciate the world around them, but also how to survive in that world. When the Haudenosaunee (Iroquois) imagined the North Wind as a great bear, they were warning their children of the danger such a cold wind brings. When the Yana people told their story about Flint Boy losing his dog, they were teaching the consequences of neglect.

These poems also demonstrate the ability of the Native Americans to describe their world in a poetic way, using metaphor with great skill. For instance, you'll see in this collection a rainbow is described as a hanging pack strap and shooting stars are likened to swiftly darting birds.

Of course, what you are reading are not the original words Native people spoke or sang. These poems are based on English translations. A true Lakota song about the wind would have much more repetition and sound very different. For example, the following song, recorded by the ethnologist Frances Densmore, comes from a Lakota singer named Siya'ka about a hundred years ago:

toki tate uye-cin	where the wind is blowing
tate ica'limunyan	the wind is roaring
nawa'zin ye	I stand
wiyo'lipeyata	to the west
tate uye'cin	the wind is blowing
tate ica'limunyan	the wind is roaring
nawa'zin ye	I stand

While WHIRLWIND IS A SPIRIT DANCING is an enjoyable collection of stories and images based on Native American traditions, it can also be a starting point towards the appreciation of the depth and variety of American Indian oral traditions. I hope it will inspire all its readers to want to learn more about these fascinating people.

— **Joseph Bruchac**, winner of the Lifetime Achievement Award from the Native Writers Circle of the Americas

Whirlwind is a spirit
That whirls and turns,
Twists in fleet moccasins,
Sweeps up dust spinning
Across the dry flatlands.

Whirlwind
Is a spirit dancing.

Lakota (Sioux)
North and South Dakota

In the beginning there was no earth.
There was only water and Turtle floating about
    on a raft.

One day Earth-Initiate dropped down
    on a feathered rope from the sky.
Turtle said to him, "I am tired of floating about."

Earth-Initiate told Turtle,
    "Dive to the bottom. Bring up dirt between your nails."

Earth-Initiate scraped that dirt from Turtle's nails,
Fastened it to the sky with four long ropes,
Formed it into a round shape,
Laid it on Turtle's raft.

That shape stretched out. It became the earth.
Turtle sat on it and basked.

Maidu
California

The sky is a bowl of ice
Turned over above the earth.

The rainbow is a great snake
Rubbing his back against the ice,
Shedding his skin in bits of snow and rain.

Neme (Shoshone)
Nevada and Utah

A man sits in the ice
Northward from here,
Holds the earth between his outstretched legs
With ropes.

Sometimes the earth slips.
He tightens the ropes to steady it.

For a moment, the earth shakes.

Nuxalk (Bella Coola)
British Columbia

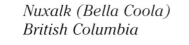

Moon sits smoking his pipe.
Night after clear night he sits smoking,
And the clouds are the smoke from his pipe.

When rain is coming, or snow,
He lays out a hoop around himself,
A circle of frozen smoke,
Builds a house for himself on its frame,
Sits in the doorway smoking
Until the snow begins, or the rain.

Ntlakapamux (Thompson River)
British Columbia

Digger Boy was hunting clams.
He cried because he could not find enough
   to fill his basket.
"If you do not stop crying, the moon will take
   you away,"
His sister told him. Four times she told him.

Digger Boy cried.

Moon came down, carried him off.
The shadows on the moon are Digger Boy
   with his basket.

Heiltsuk (Bella Bella)
British Columbia

Dew Eagle lives above the clouds,
Collects the dew in his feathers.
He carries a pool of water on his back.
At night he spreads cooling dew
    over the hot earth.

Haudenosaunee (Iroquois)
New York

Not long after the earth was made
And men and birds and animals came upon it,
The sun traveled low in the sky.
Bear's white coat was burned black,
Grizzly Bear's coat was scorched.

So Earth-Maker's son raised mountains
To fence the sun safely away.

Nuxalk (Bella Coola)
British Columbia

Before men came up from below the earth
    to live,
The Mother-of-Men made the stars;
Made them of cornmeal dough
And did not bake them
So that the cornmeal would shine yellow
    in the sky.

Cochiti Pueblo
New Mexico

Sun rays shining through the dusty air,
Breaking through the rain clouds,
Are Earth-Maker's eyelashes.

Nuxalk (Bella Coola)
British Columbia

The chief of the world
Lives above the earth
In the Council House,
The invisible house
In which everything was begun,
The house where the carpenters made man
And the animals and birds,
Made all that lives,
The house to which man goes when he dies.

The sun is the chief's canoe.

Nuxalk (Bella Coola)
British Columbia

First Man and First Woman
Decorated the mountains;
Fastened them with bolts of lighting
And sunbeams
And rainbows.

Made headdresses for them
Of dove feathers,
The feathers of bluebirds
And blackbirds and yellow warblers.

Wrapped them in cloud blankets
Blue and yellow and white and black.
Adorned them with crystal
And turquoise and jet
And haliotis shell.

In the beginning
First Man and First Woman
Decorated the mountains.

Aashiwi (Zuni)
New Mexico

The stars are night birds with bright breasts
Like hummingbirds.

Twinkling stars are birds flying slowly.
Shooting stars are birds darting swiftly.

Taos Pueblo
New Mexico

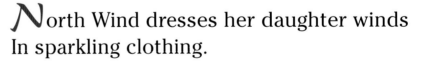

North Wind dresses her daughter winds
In sparkling clothing.

East Wind's daughters are jealous.
They melt the snow-fur blankets.
They tear the icicle pendants.
They tangle the frost-feather headdresses

Until North Wind's daughters hide
Weeping, in their mother's lodge.

Tlingi
Alaska

The northern lights are the flames
  and the smoke
From the fires of the dwarfs
Cooking seal and walrus meat.

Makah
Washington

Lightning is a great giant
Who makes a path through the sky
For the thunderstorm.

His bonnet is feathered clouds.
His blanket is a black cloud.
His moccasins are the swift winds.

He carries the whirlwind like a sack
  slung over his shoulder.
He whips the clouds with his lariat.

Skidi Pawnee
Nebraska

Flint Boy tied his dog.
Left him shut in the lodge when he went hunting.

Flint Boy's wife untied the dog,
Let him leave the lodge because he barked,
Wanting to go hunting.

Flint Boy's dog ran up the mountain,
Called clouds to come for him,
Climbed on the back of a storm cloud,
Wrapped himself in a black cloud,
Went away because Flint Boy would not
    take him hunting.

Thunder is Flint Boy's dog
Barking.

Yana
California

The winds are people dwelling,
Spirits guarding the four corners of the sky.

East Wind is Moose running,
Rushing, stamping about,
Breathing in wet gusts.

South Wind is Doe starting up from her drinking,
Moving swiftly from the brook,
Softly through the meadow
Into the shaded wood,
Hurrying to her fawn.

West Wind is Panther whining,
Angry, threatening Bobcat and Lynx,
Spoiling for a fight.

North Wind is Bear prowling,
Climbing the longhouse roof,
Uncovering the smoke holes,
Reaching down with cold paws
To scatter the fires.

Haudenosaunee (Iroquois)
New York

Springs do not freeze in the cold of winter.
They bubble up through the snow
And no ice forms on them,
For their water comes up from the Land of the Ghosts
Below, where men speak only in yawns
And canoes are without bottoms
And winter never comes.

Nuxalk (Bella Coola)
British Columbia

Frost is an old man walking in the woods.
He raps the trees with his club,
And men in their lodges hear the sharp
    cracking blows.

Haudenosaunee (Iroquois)
New York

Icicles are the walking sticks of the winter winds.

Nuxalk (Bella Coola)
British Columbia

Glous'gap's wigwam
Once stood with the wigwams of men,
And men learned from him
How to raise corn, how to fish,
How to fashion bows and arrows
And to hunt with them.
They learned about the stars.
Whatever they needed to know,
Glous'gap taught men.

Then he moved his wigwam
Far away beyond a high mountain
On a road guarded by serpents
And hidden by clouds.

But men know they have nothing to fear
When they see the rainbow:
Glous'gap is home in his wigwam;
He is watching the homes of men.
He has hung up his packstrap as a sign.

Micmac
New Brunswick and Nova Scotia

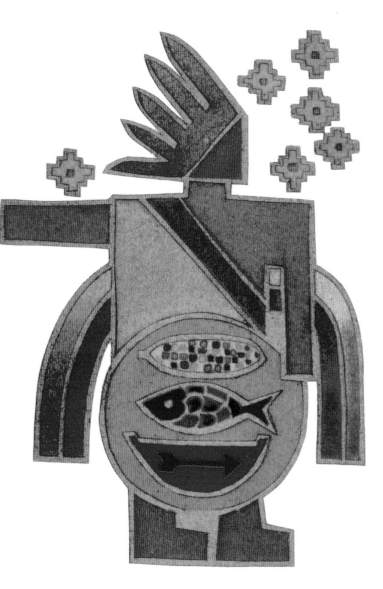

The sun is a yellow-tipped porcupine
Lolloping through the sky,
Nibbling treetops and grasses and weeds,
Floating in rivers and ponds,
Casting shining barbed quills at the earth.

Absaroke (Crow)
Montana

Aashiwi (Zuni)

New Mexico: Zuni Pueblo is one of the oldest farming communities in the United States. The Zuni town of Hawikah was first visited by Europeans in 1540.

Absaroke (Crow)

Montana: The Absaroke or "Bird People" are among the plains nations of people who relied on the hunting of the buffalo. Early allies of the Americans during the Revolutionary War, the tipis of the Absaroke were the tallest on the plains.

Cochiti Pueblo

New Mexico: Like the other pueblos of the Rio Grande valley, the people of Cochiti have long been skillful farmers, developing crops that can survive in the arid southwest.

Haudenosaunee (Iroquois)

New York: The Haudenosaunee or "People of the Longhouse" gained their name from their long, multi-family, bark-covered houses. The government of the five nations that made up their "League of Peace" has been cited as a major influence on the United States Constitution.

Heiltsuk (Bella Bella)

British Columbia: The Heiltsuk, whose name means "Native People," practiced a culture similar to that of their neighbors, the Nuxalk, though their language is quite different. Fishing, hunting and gathering are important to them, as is their continued protection of the rivers and land through both ceremony and careful use.

Lakota (Sioux)

North and South Dakota: No native nations have become more emblematic of American Indian culture than the Lakotas. Their clothing, their buffalo hunting, and even their language is most often portrayed in movies and art.

Maidu

California: Like many of the other Native people of California, the Maidu migrated seasonally from the high country to the valleys, hunting, fishing and gathering acorns from the bountiful land given to them by a kindly creator.

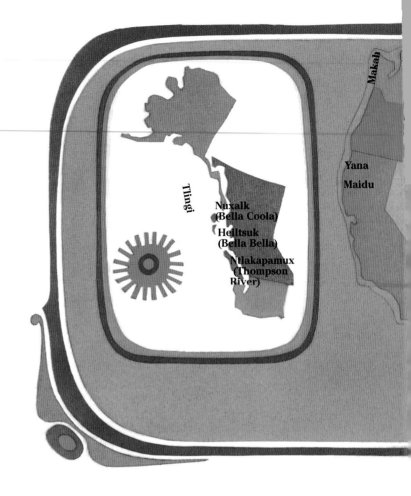

Makah

Washington: The Makah have a great tradition as skilled mariners, using various types of cedar canoes, some of which were very large and employed sails. From salmon to seals to whales, the creatures of the ocean have long meant life to the Makahs.

Micmac

New Brunswick and Nova Scotia: The Micmacs remain the most numerous of the Wabanaki or "Dawn land" peoples, with more than 20,000 in the maritime provinces. Many still practice the seasonal round of hunting and coastal fishing that has been their way of life for thousands of years.

Nuxalk (Bella Coola)

British Columbia: Fishing remains the primary way of life for these coastal people of British Columbia who live near the mouth of the Bella Coola River. Famous for their wood carving and rich ceremonies, their traditional dwellings were cedar plank houses.

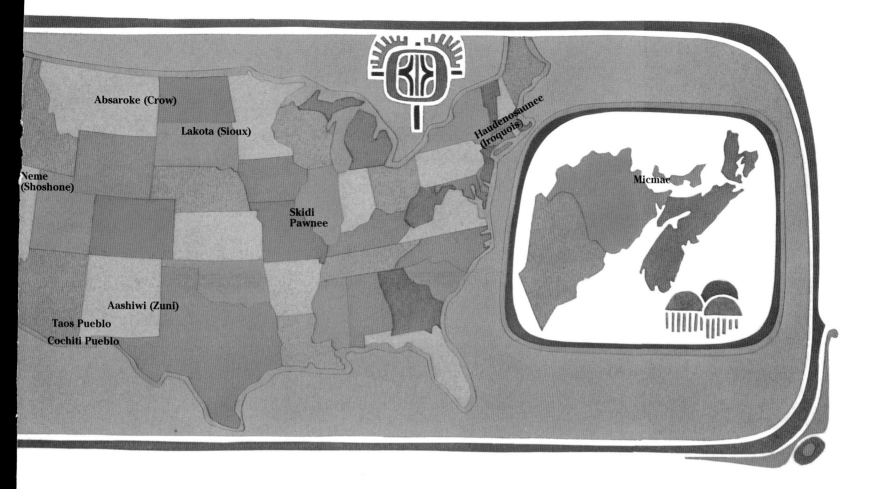

Ntlakapamux (Thompson River)

British Columbia: Commonly known by the name of the river that flows through their territory, the Ntlakapamux have long relied on the sock-eye salmon as a mainstay of their food supply.

Neme (Shoshone)

Nevada and Utah: The Neme, whose name means "Human Beings," were among the many native nations whose way of life changed forever with the arrival of the horse in the 19th century, giving them power and prestige as hunters and horse breeders.

Skidi Pawnee

Nebraska: The Pawnee name for themselves is Chahiksichahks, meaning "men of men." The Skidi or "Wolves" are one of their four main groups. They formerly lived in earth-lodge villages, relying on both hunting and growing corn.

Taos Pueblo

New Mexico: More than 500 years old, Taos is the most heavily visited of the New Mexico pueblos. Its picturesque multi-story buildings have been the subject of countless artists.

Tlingi

Alaska: The Tlingits have long been the dominant people of Southeastern Alaska, where they gained a reputation as skilled fishermen and fair traders.

Yana

California: The hunting and gathering way of life of the Yana people was best described by Ishi, a "Yahi" Indian who was regarded as the last of his people. Once thought to be extinct, a large group of Yana people who still speak their own language remain in northern California.

A publication of
Milk & Cookies Press, a division of ibooks, inc.

Distributed by Publishers Group West
1700 Fourth Street, Berkeley, CA 94710

ibooks, inc.
24 West 25th Street, 11th floor, New York, NY 10010

ISBN: 1-59687-173-3
First ibooks, inc. printing: April 2006
10 9 8 7 6 5 4 3 2 1

Editor - Dinah Dunn
Associate Editor - Robin Bader

Designed by Edie Weinberg

Library of Congress Cataloging-in-Publication Data available

Manufactured in China